The Adventures of Penrose
the mathematical cat

by theoni pappas

— Wide World Publishing/Tetra —

Wide World Publishing/Tetra
P.O. Box 476
San Carlos, CA 94070

Published in the United States of America by Wide World Publishing
Manufactured in China by DIYA USA

10th Printing October 2011

Library of Congress Cataloging-in-Publication Data
Pappas, Theoni
        The adventures of Penrose : The mathematical cat / by Theoni
    Pappas .
                p.   cm.
        Summary : Penrose the cat explores and experiences a variety of
mathematical concepts, including infinity, the golden rectangle, and
impossible figures.
    ISBN 1- 884550-14-2 (alk. paper)
    1. Mathematics -- Study and teaching (Elementary)
[1 . Mathematics.]   1. Title .
QA135.5.P332   1997
510--dc21   97-41182
                                                            CIP
                                                             AC

For Lucy & Penrose

TABLE OF CONTENTS

TABLE OF CONTENTS continued

Preface

How is it that a cat came to be interested in mathematics? Let me try to explain. One day I had been working on a project. My living room floor was strewn with notes on mathematics. When I left the room momentarily to answer the telephone, my kitten Penrose wandered in. Being a very

curious kitten he headed directly for the center of my project. He immediately started pushing a pencil with his paw, and began nuzzling my notes and rubbing his nose all over them. Penrose joyously stretched out on top of the

papers while playing with the pencil. Entering the room and seeing this sight, I couldn't resist taking photos of Penrose's introduction to mathematics. From that day on this cat has constantly been invading my desk, my books, my mathematical models. Whenever I put papers down, Penrose will most certainly arrive. It seems it has almost become a game. Or has it? The escapades of Penrose within this book will help you make up your mind. Penrose has sparked my imagination, perhaps he will do the same for you.

—Theoni Pappas

Penrose meets the 0s and 1s

It was one of those days when Penrose had spent too much time looking at his mistress' math books.

His eyes were heavy, and before he knew it he had drifted off to sleep. He found himself in a place full of only zeros and ones.

"What are all you zeros and ones doing here?" Penrose asked. "I've never seen so many zeros and ones gathered in groups before."

"We are not just zeros and ones. We can represent any number you can think of," a zero replied.

"Do you mean you can make any number from just the digits 0 and 1? How can that be? The numbers I use to count with are 0, 1, 2, 3, 4, 5, 6, 7, 8, 9, 10, 11, 12, 13, … and so on,"

We are not just 0s and 1s!

Penrose said.

"You mean to tell us you don't know any other number systems?" they asked in astonishment.

"Welllllll nooooo," Penrose admitted timidly, which was certainly out of character.

"Believe us, there can be as many number systems as numbers, but they are not all practical. We're really special because by just using the two digits 0 and 1 and what's called <u>positional place value</u>, we can write any number."

"I'm beginning to understand," Penrose said, his eyes lighting up. "The number system I use,   which is called base 10, uses the ten digits—0,1,2,3,4,5,6,7,8,9. If I write 325, it means **3** hundreds and **2** tens and **5** ones, or we say three hundred and twenty five. So you're saying in your number system, base two, you use only two digits—0 and 1. And the different places have values related to the number 2 as base ten has them related to the number 10?"

"Exactly!" they said with sighs of relief. "So if we write 10110 it stands for 1 sixteen, 0 eights, 1 four, 1 two and 0 ones, which totals 16+0+4+2+0=22 in your base ten system. Do you get it?" the zeros and ones asked together.

"Well, yes," replied Penrose. "But who uses your numbers? They seem so strange, and of no use to me," Penrose asked, knowing his question might make them angry.

"The numbers we form are not strange. We only seem strange to you because you have never used us. If it were not for us, so many things that use electrical power and circuits would not be possible," a Zero replied. "Like what?" asked Penrose. "Like computers, telephones, televisions. Objects that are powered by electricity can only function and communicate in two modes, ON or OFF. Electricity can only be either ON or OFF. So mathematicians use the base two number system to signal and write codes using only 1s and 0s. 1 stands for ON and 0 stands for OFF," a very intellectual looking One explained.

"Now <u>that</u> makes sense. How clever and how very important your number system is," Penrose said.

"Thank you," all the ones and zeros responded. "What's your favorite number, Penrose?"

"Why, it is 5," Penrose replied. And with this a zero and some ones got into formations of 101.

A big smile came across Penrose's face, as he recognized that 101 is 5 written in base two.   (1 four + 0 twos + 1 one = 5)

If 1011 is a base two number, how is it written in base 10?

Answer is given at the back of the book.

Penrose is captured by the numbers

Penrose was having one of his usual days, lounging around his mistress' office.

The sun was beaming in, so he sashayed over and stretched out in its warmth. Before he realized it, he was catnapping. He found himself walking along a path. Up ahead he saw a faint object running toward him. Penrose could not believe his eyes— 2 was running at breakneck speed dragging a square root sign. It stopped as it approached Penrose. "Help me!" it shouted. "The whole numbers, fractions and decimals do not want me to keep this symbol."

"Why is that?" Penrose inquired.

"The moment I put this symbol over me I am no longer one of them," 2 replied.

"What do you mean, you are no longer one of them?" Penrose asked.

Help me! The whole numbers, fractions and decimals do not want me to keep this symbol.

"I don't have time to explain. You must hide this before they destroy it," 2 pleaded frantically, handing Penrose the square root symbol. "They'll be here any minute. Please help."

Penrose took the square root sign, cautiously placing it on the ground. Then he stretched out on it, covering it with his body. Within a moment hundreds of other numbers came running toward him and 2, shouting, "Where is it? Where is it?" Penrose and 2 pretended not to understand

what they were talking about. The crowd of numbers was getting angrier and angrier. Their leader, 1, shouted "SURROUND THEM!" And before they knew it the numbers had encircled Penrose and 2.

Penrose tried to remain calm. In a quiet but firm voice he said, "There must be some mistake here."

"You bet there is a mistake. You made the mistake of hiding the square root symbol," 1 contended.

"Why do you want the symbol, and what do you plan to do with it?" Penrose asked.

"We plan to destroy it," they all shouted at once.

"But, why?" Penrose prodded.

"Because when that square root symbol is placed on some of us, strange numbers are formed. Numbers unlike any of us. As we stand now, each and every one of us can be expressed as a fraction, in which the numerator and denominator are whole numbers. For example, 7 can be written as 7/1, the number 0.25 can be written as

Family? We are in the same family with THOSE numbers?

That's what I was trying to explain to all of you.

6

25/100 or 1/4, and the number 3 1/2 can be changed to 7/3. Even .6767676767... can be changed to 67/99," 1 explained. "BUT 2, with the square root symbol over it, becomes a never ending non-repeating decimal."

"I know all that," Penrose replied, "but haven't you heard of the irrational numbers."

"Irrationals?" they asked.

"Don't you know that YOU, the rationals and numbers such as √2, √3, √5, √7, √10,... and π and others – which are called irrationals – belong to a family called the real numbers?" Penrose explained.

"Family? We are in the same family with THOSE numbers?" They looked astonished.

"That's what I was trying to explain to all you of," 2 interjected. "The square root symbol both helps us discover new relatives and solves problems which are impossible to solve without the irrationals."

"What type of problems?" skeptical 3 asked.

" None of you is the answer to the problem,

What number times itself equals 5. OR can any of you be used to express the length of the diagonal of a 1 by 1 square? Here's where irrational numbers come to the rescue because √5 is the answer to ?x?=5."

Penrose suddenly felt someone trying to pull the square root sign from under him. To his surprise, it was his mistress pulling her papers with square root problems written on them.

Here are some square root problems to try.
example: √9 =3 because 3 x 3 = 9.

(1) √16 = ?

(2) √49 = ?

(3) √? = 5

(4) √1 = ?

(5) √? = 8

(6) Can you express the number √8 as a fraction?

The answers to these are at the back of the book in the solutions section.

Penrose discovers mathematical stars

Have you ever started to play with

something and then made a discovery? This is what happened to Penrose the day his mistress left the polygonal models she had

You are just polygons.

What's the big idea sitting on us?

Get off of us! Don't you know who we are?

just finished making for one of her class presentations on her desk. Penrose loved to stretch out on her desk because he knew she would return eventually and would pet him. He curled up on one of the piles

Just polygons? How dare you!

of models she had made. As he lay there he heard voices yelling—"You're squashing us!" "Please get off of us." "Your fur is going to make me sneeze." And with that a giant "KKKKAAAAA-CCCHH HHOOOOO" sounded, making Penrose jump. The polygons stood upright. "What's the big idea? Don't you know who we are?" they asked indignantly in unison. "Why, you are just polygons," Penrose replied.

"JUST? We are the producers of mathematical stars," one pentagon shouted. And immediately a pentagram formed inside the pentagon. Penrose was totally startled. "That's tricky," he declared. "It's more than tricky, it is magnificent," the hexagon

chimed in and amazingly a six-pointed star formed in the hexagon. Then the heptagon, the octagon , the nonagon , the decagon, in fact, all the gons started forming their stars. These beautiful stars were effortlessly forming within the polygons surrounding Penrose. "That's truly amazing. By drawing a segment on every other vertex, a star is formed. May I try making a mathematical star on you," Penrose asked the nonagon.

"Welllllll all right, but see if you notice how different stars form

We're the producers of mathematical stars!

for even and odd sided polygons," the nonagon challenged Penrose. "Yes, I see what you mean," Penrose replied, with an appreciative note to his voice. "I've also noticed how to tell how many points each polygon's star will have."

Try it out for yourself, and discover what Penrose found.

The answer is given at the back of the book in the solutions section

9

Penrose discovers pancake world

Penrose always felt especially curious when the moon was full.

Tonight was one of those nights. Jumping up on the back fence, he peered down and noticed a hole in the ground he had never seen before. It was a large deep hole with no end in sight. "A perfect adventure for a full moon night," Penrose thought as he slowly entered the hole. After his tail had cleared the opening, he rubbed his paws over his eyes. He was startled by the brightness of the new world he had entered. "My goodness," he thought, "what have I stumbled into?" There were creatures whose shapes he had not known existed. Everything was so very flat. He saw something that was shaped like a large hexagon, and picked it up. He suddenly heard something, shaped like a triangle, Δ, screaming, "My house! My house! What's

My house! My house! What's happening to my house?

10

happened to my house?" Penrose immediately put it back. And the Δ calmed down. "What's the matter?" Penrose asked the Δ. The Δ addressed Penrose's paws, saying "My house disappeared for a moment."

"That's ridiculous. Didn't you see me pick it up?" Penrose replied. "Up?" said the Δ, "What is up?" "UP is up here," said Penrose. But the Δ, still looking at Penrose's paws, had a confused expression and responded, "There is no such thing or word in the world as UP." "What about the word down?" said Penrose. "DOWN?" said the Δ, with a blank look about it.

Penrose's tail was pointing straight up as his curiosity increased. He asked the Δ, "Where am I?" The Δ replied, "You are in Pancake World." "Pancake World?" asked Penrose. "Yes," repeated the Δ, "Pancake World."

Then Penrose asked, "When you speak to me, why do you talk to my paws?"

"Where should I address you?" asked the Δ.

"Up here," replied Penrose. "Up?" said the Δ. "Do you know the meaning of right and left?" asked Penrose.

"Yes, of course," replied the Δ.

"What about the words forward , backward, and sideways?" Penrose asked.

Again the Δ replied, "Yes."

Penrose thought a moment, and then asked, "What about the words in and out ? "

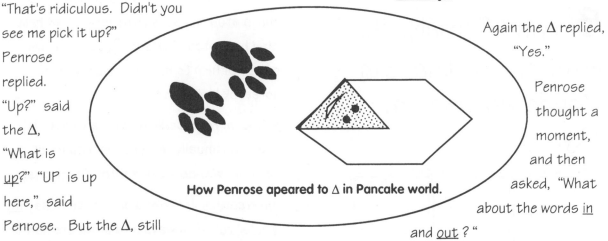

How Penrose apeared to Δ in Pancake world.

"What do the words in or out mean?" asked the Δ.

Now Penrose realized where he was and why the Δ only talked to his paws. He understood how he had made the hexagon house disappear and reappear to the Δ.

Suddenly Penrose felt himself being lifted up. He opened his eyes and realized his mistress was lifting him from her geometry book on which he had fallen asleep while reading the pages on 2-dimensional objects.

The solutions and answers section at the end of the book talks about what Penrose discovered.

Penrose meets the fractal dragon

Blowing fiercely, the wind moved the rain clouds across the sky.

In no time, the sun was completely hidden by the clouds. Penrose put his paws on the windowsill and peered outside. "There is no way I am going out today," he complained. "I'll just snuggle down next to my mistress' computer notes."

"F-r-a-c-t-a-l," he pronounced slowly. "So she is studying something new. I had better read her notes while she is out. That way I can be of help to her," he thought. In her notebook he began to read:

A fractal repeatedly follows a rule and thus continually reproduces copies of itself in various sizes and/or directions.

"Interesting! If I take a square and I say <u>my fractal rule is</u> **always add a square half the size of the last one drawn at its upper left corner,** would this be a fractal?" he thought. It should be because it always follows my rule. I suppose I could have decided to add a square that is always double the size of the last one drawn, then the fractal would grow outward." So Penrose quickly drew a picture of his fractal.

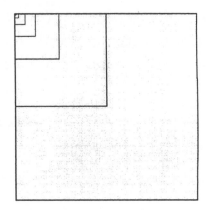

"What does one do with fractals?" Penrose wondered, as he read on.

Fractals can be used to describe the many shapes of our world. Examples include

clouds, mountains, plants, trees, rocks. A mathematician devises a rule and lets mathematics do the rest.

"Hmmmm, most interesting," Penrose concluded, but now it's time for a cat nap." Just as he was drifting off to sleep,

something made his eyes spring open. A dragon had entered the room.

Startled, Penrose asked, "Where did you come from?"

"I am a fractal dragon. I jumped from your mistress' computer screen," the dragon replied.

"But you're growing and changing before my eyes," Penrose shouted.

"I know," replied the dragon. "That is what fractals do. They continually grow and change. I was getting tired of being confined to the computer's monitor. I needed to blow off some steam." Suddenly, smoke spewed from his mouth.

"Soon this room won't be big enough for you," Penrose said, a bit frightened. Remembering what he had just read about fractals, he asked, "What's your rule?"

The dragon repeated his rule. Hearing it, Penrose immediately grabbed the dragon's tail and began to reverse its rule. To Penrose's amazement the dragon began to shrink.

The dragon was frightened that it might shrink into nothing, so by holding onto its remaining parts it jumped back into the computer monitor, and saved itself at just that stage.

"And I thought the storm was scary," Penrose said. "I had no idea there were mathematical monsters. I think I'll go out and get some fresh air after all." So declaring, Penrose cheerfully leaped through his cat door and headed outdoors into the stormy day.

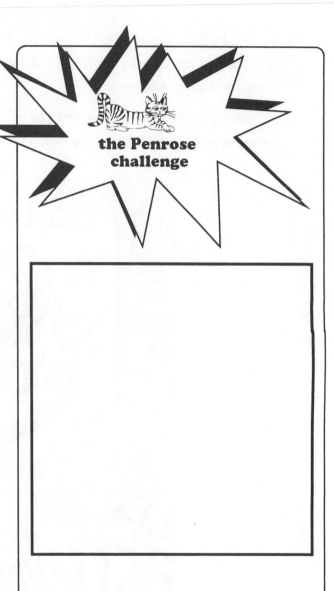

the Penrose challenge

(1) With a ruler make a square like the one above. Using this square form a fractal by following this rule:

> **At each of the square's corners, place a square whose sides are 1/3 the size of the previous square.**

(A drawing of the 4th stage of this fractal is given in the solutions section at the end of the book.)

(2) Try designing your own fractal.

Here are some of the stages in the formation of a dragon fractal. The dotted line is removed, after it is replaced with two sides of half a square.

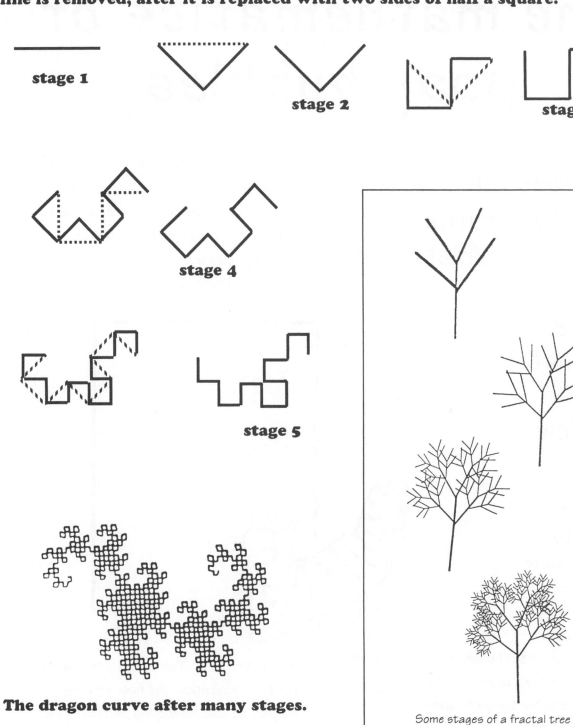

stage 1

stage 2

stage 3

stage 4

stage 5

The dragon curve after many stages.

Some stages of a fractal tree

Penrose discovers the mathematics of soap bubbles

Penrose was startled out of his catnap when the rain started to patter against the window near where he lay. "Another indoor day," Penrose thought sadly. He rose and slowly walked into the adjoining room. Round balls were moving all around the room. "What are these things floating by my nose?" he wondered. "He watched as his mistress dipped one of many different

wands into a solution and drew it through the air. Wanting to have a closer look, he dashed over by her side. Raising a paw to touch one of the transparent balls made it suddenly disappear into thin air. Just then the doorbell rang, and his mistress went to

answer the door. Penrose walked toward the bowl of solution. The floor was so slippery he lost his footing and fell head first into the bowl, and then flipped high into the air. Before he realized what had happened, Penrose was floating in a transparent bubble. "What a ride!" he marvelled. In a split second the bubble burst and he tumbled down feet first into a cluster of bubbles. "What's the big idea?" the bubbles started shouting at him. "I was just trying to learn about you," Penrose said apologetically.

"The best way to learn about us is to do what your mistress was doing—experimenting with soap bubbles. Pick-up any wand and dip it into the soap solution. Then either blow air into the wand or whisk it through the air," they replied.

Penrose picked-up the circular shaped wand, and out came spherical bubbles like the ones he had been seeing. "Oh! I see," he said jumping to a conclusion. "Your shapes change with the shape of the wand." "Wrong!" the bubbles shouted. "Try another wand."

This time he took the triangular wand, expecting a pyramid shape to emerge. But to his surprise another spherical bubble formed. A bit disturbed by this, Penrose then picked-up the square wand, but a cube bubble didn't appear. Again it was a sphere. "How can this be?" Penrose asked.

"Nature conserves its resources, and the sphere's shape encloses the most space for the least surface area. That is why all single bubbles are spheres," the bubbles explained.

"Fascinating!" Penrose said, astonished. "What happens when bubbles are not alone?" Penrose asked.

"Look at the cluster of us closely. What do you see?"

"I seem to see bubbles squashed together," Penrose said, with a questioning note to his voice.

"Study your mistress' 2-dimensional drawing of a layer of bubbles and pencil in heavy dots wherever the circles meet. Do you see something familiar?" they asked.

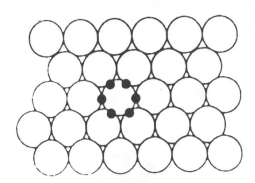

Penrose looked, and suddenly he purred and declared, "I see hexagons!" and proceeded to draw some on his mistress' sketch.

"That's right! When we come together in clusters of bubbles, we make what is called a triple junction, three 120° angles. Regular hexagons fit together perfectly, leaving no gaps. They tessellate a plane. The same idea is true of bubble clusters, but in a 3-dimensional form."

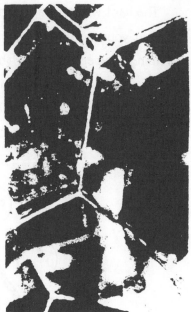

"I never knew bubbles were so mathematical," Penrose marveled.

"There is even more math in soap film, but we are about ready to dissolve. See you next time Penrose." And the cluster of bubbles burst just as Penrose's mistress returned.

She picked-up her notebook, and was puzzled as she looked at it. "I don't remember drawing those dots in this sketch," she mused. Penrose had curled into a ball of fur, hoping his mistress would not

think he had done anything. She looked down
at Penrose and wondered for just a moment.
And then immediately put the thought out
of her mind.

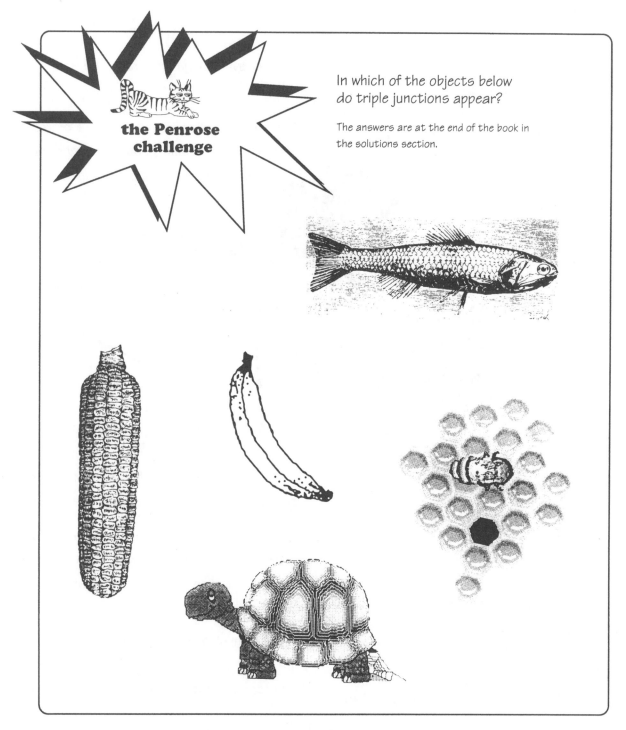

the Penrose challenge

In which of the objects below
do triple junctions appear?

The answers are at the end of the book in
the solutions section.

Penrose learns the truth about infinity

"I am Infinity," the deep voice declared. "No one can catch me. I am never ending."

"But what are you?" asked Penrose, startled from his nap.

"I am something much too difficult for you mere Earthlings to understand," Infinity replied.

"Well, try," Penrose said, trying to sound self assured.

"This should be amusing," the voice continued. "I have always been, but not always known to you Earthlings. I am an idea that can be used with many things—objects, numbers, points. I am a quantity that cannot be grasped. You might

But what are you?

say I always change and grow. I have no end."

This explanation seemed to confuse Penrose even more. He became impatient and asked, "Please give me specific examples."

"Examples, you want!" Infinity sneered. "I am the number of points on this line segment and the length of any line. I am the number of

counting numbers, the number of integers, the number of fractions. I am the number of numbers between 0 and 1/2."

"Just a minute," Penrose interrupted. "From your other examples I see you are a gigantic object, but there can't be that many numbers between 0 and 1/2."

"Oh Earthling, have you forgotten about 1/3, 1/4, 1/5, 1/6, 1/7, 1/8, 1/9, 1/10, 1/11, et cetera, et cetera, et cetera?" Infinity replied smugly.

"Aha! I see," Penrose said, his eyes lighting up. "Anything that has no boundaries is infinite."

"No!" Infinity said, a bit irritated. "0 and 1/2 are boundaries for the numbers between them. The the endpoints of a line segment are also boundaries for the points on a segment."

"So a thing is infinite if it never runs out of the objects that make it up," Penrose blurted. "And you can cover a large space or a small space, as a line segment, just so long as there is always another one of it after the last one mentioned. I know this sounds like double talk, but that's what you are, aren't you?"

"I am INFINITY— no more, no less, INFINITY, INFINITY,INFINITY…" the deep voice replied, its words echoing and fading away.

Penrose took the line segment drawn on a piece of paper. He curled up on top of the paper. He knew he had caught an infinity, and he was resting on top of it.

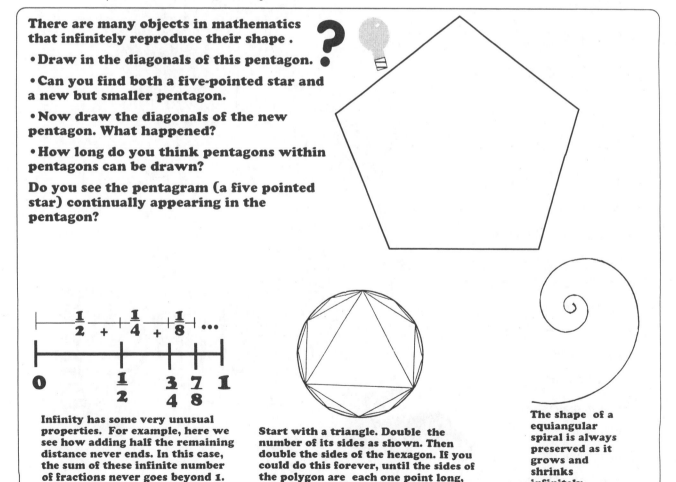

There are many objects in mathematics that infinitely reproduce their shape .

• **Draw in the diagonals of this pentagon.**

• **Can you find both a five-pointed star and a new but smaller pentagon.**

• **Now draw the diagonals of the new pentagon. What happened?**

• **How long do you think pentagons within pentagons can be drawn?**

Do you see the pentagram (a five pointed star) continually appearing in the pentagon?

$$\frac{1}{2} + \frac{1}{4} + \frac{1}{8} \ \cdots$$

0    $\frac{1}{2}$ $\frac{3}{4}$ $\frac{7}{8}$ 1

Infinity has some very unusual properties. For example, here we see how adding half the remaining distance never ends. In this case, the sum of these infinite number of fractions never goes beyond 1.

Start with a triangle. Double the number of its sides as shown. Then double the sides of the hexagon. If you could do this forever, until the sides of the polygon are each one point long, the result would be a circle.

The shape of a equiangular spiral is always preserved as it grows and shrinks infinitely.

Penrose meets Fibonacci rabbit

"The wonderful thing about my neighborhood," Penrose thought, "is that one gets to meet so many interesting creatures.

In fact, I'll never forget the day I ran into Fibonacci rabbit." Until that day Penrose thought he was the only creature in the animal kingdom that loved to study mathematics.

On that special day many years ago, Penrose was stretched out under some sunflowers that were in full bloom. Something caught his eye as it moved in small leaps and hops. He had never seen anything like it before. At first he was going to chase it away because he thought it was eating his mistress' plants, but to his surprise it was taking notes. Before he knew it, the creature had leaped over next to him—well, actually next to the sunflowers. "What are you doing?" asked Penrose.

discover the special Fibonacci numbers. Surely you have read about me?" the rabbit asked.

"Fibonacci numbers?' Penrose thought aloud. "Which are they?"

" 1, 1, 2, 3, 5, and 8 and 13 and 21 and on and on," the rabbit replied.

"They seem like regular numbers to me," Penrose countered.

"Fibonacci numbers? Which are they?"

They are the numbers 1,1,2,3,5, and 8 and 13 and 21 and on and on.

"Oh!" said the rabbit, "I'm just gathering some information for a book I'm writing."

"Book?" Penrose asked skeptically.

"Yes. I am Fibonacci, the famous rabbit that Fibonacci the mathematican used to

"True, they are numbers you have seen, heard and used; but what makes these famous is how they are arranged. Do you notice the pattern?" the rabbit asked with a note of excitement in its voice. "Any number is the sum of the two numbers before it."

"Oh! I see," Penrose exclaimed. "Two equals one plus one. Five equals two plus three and so on."

"Right!" Fibonacci said.

"But surely they are not just famous for that pattern?" Penrose asked.

"You're right," Fibonacci replied. "I first discovered these numbers when I was studying reproduction patterns of different rabbits. And a hypothetical problem I proposed produced these numbers. Then I was especially fascinated to find that this pattern of numbers appears in all sorts of places in nature."

"Please tell me," Penrose asked eagerly.

"Look, for instance, at the seedhead of this sunflower near you." Fibonacci pointed. "See how there are two directions of spiralling seeds. Counting the number that spiral to the right and the number to the left we find 8 and 13. Notice these numbers are consecutive Fibonacci numbers."

"Wow!" Penrose blurted.

"And that's just the beginning," continued Fibonacci. "You find Fibonacci numbers in a similar way in pinecones, pineapples, artichokes, and seedheads of many other flowers. The petal count of many types of flowers, such as daisies and iris, happen to be Fibonacci numbers. Even the way leaves grow on a stem or branch can illustrate Fibonacci numbers. See how these numbers can appear on stems," he said,

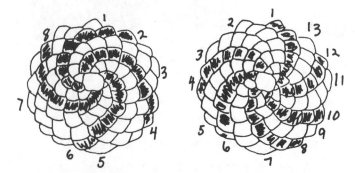

This pinecone has 8 spirals turning to the right and 13 spirals turning to the left. 8 and 13 are two consecutive Fibonacci numbers.

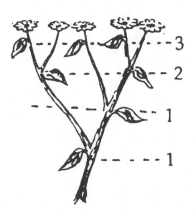

See the Fibonacci numbers appearing in the growth pattern of the leaves of this plant.

pointing to some nearby flower stems.

"Fibonacci numbers appear in many places besides plants, but we'll have to discuss that another day.   For now I must get back

to work." And Fibonacci rabbit went leaping away.

the Penrose challenge

Can you find Fibonacci numbers in the flower below?

The answers are at the end of the book in the solutions section.

cosmos
number of petals ____

trillium
number of petals ____

wild rose
number of petals ____

bloodroot
number of petals ____

Penrose watches the puzzling egg hatch

"**W**hat a beautiful sunny day," Penrose thought as he lay stretched out under a tree in the backyard.

The sun warming his body made him drowsy, and in no time he was in a deep sleep.

An annoying tap, tap tap sound woke Penrose. Without moving his body, he opened his eyes. To his surprise there were a bunch of strange birds all around the yard tapping with their beaks on nine geometric objects.

"What are you doing?" Penrose asked.

"We are trying to figure out how to put this egg back together," they replied in unison.

"I do not see an egg," Penrose said. "I see nine geometric pieces."

The bird with the big beak spoke. "Each of us hatched from eggs with nine pieces."

"Can one of you explain this more clearly?" Penrose asked.

This time the bird with the tassel on its head spoke. "Look very carefully Penrose, and I'll reveal my nine pieces." And suddenly the bird divided into nine pieces.

"Amazing!" Penrose said in awe. "Each of you is made from nine pieces like these."

"That's what we just said," the big beaked bird replied in an irritated tone. "Unless the egg is put back together, it cannot hatch."

"I think I can help put the egg back together," Penrose said. Penrose began pushing the nine pieces around with his paw, and in no time had formed them into an egg.

• Try it for yourself. See if you can fit the pieces together into an egg.

• Can you figure out how the nine pieces were put together to form each of the five birds above?

• Using all nine pieces of the egg, design your own bird.

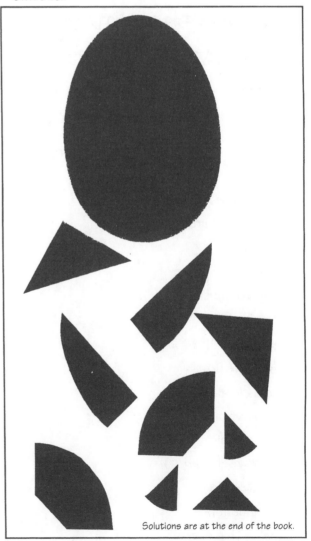

Solutions are at the end of the book.

The polyhedra connect with Penrose

"Home alone," Penrose thought out loud. As he walked slowly into the other room, he saw the door to his mistress' office closed.

"I wonder if there's something interesting in there today behind the door," Penrose speculated. It wasn't the first time a closed door kept him from exercising his curiosity. He had perfected his technique for opening this special

bifold door. Just a push with both paws on the hinge and the door opened in the middle. Penrose pushed, but nothing happened. Then he pushed really hard, and the door collapsed in the middle, as it had in the past. "Wow! Now I know why the door was closed. Her desk is full of all sorts of polyhedra solids," he said, as he looked in amazement. There were prisms, pyramids, the Platonic solids, truncated polyhedra. Penrose's eyes got really wide. While he

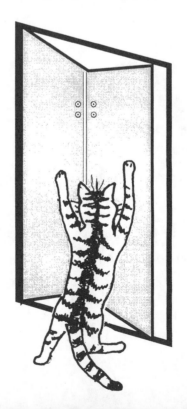

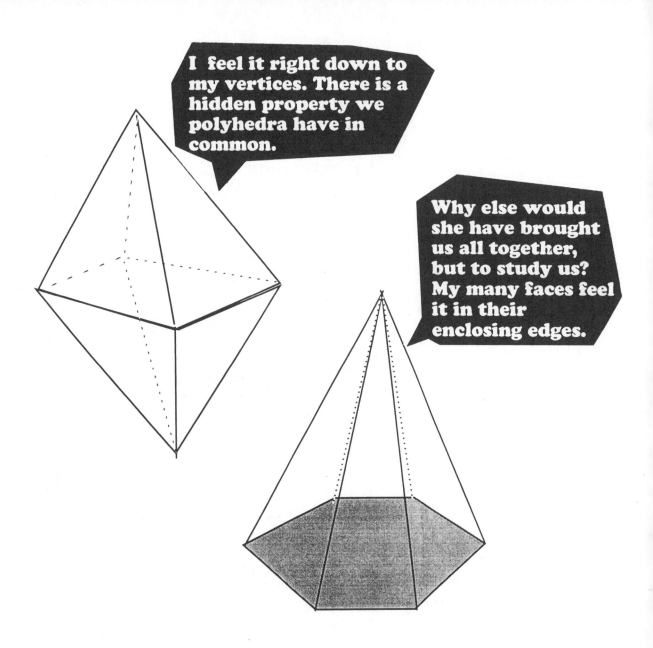

stood there staring and marveling at the shapes, he heard voices...

"I feel it right down to my vertices. There is a hidden property we polyhedra have in common," the octahedron said to a pyramid.

"I know what you mean. Why else would she have brought us all together, but to study us. My many faces feel it in their enclosing edges," the pyramid added.

"But what could it be? We all come in so many different forms. How could we have a common property? I just don't know what the connection could be," a cube wondered out loud.

"Perhaps I can help you," Penrose said. All the polyhedra jumped, when they heard his

29

voice. "We thought we were by ourselves. Besides, how can a cat discover such a mysterious mathematical property?" the tetrahedron asked. "I can get help from my friends," Penrose said with a little purr coming from his belly. "Please try," the octahedron pleaded.

*   *   *

Help Penrose discover the mysterious property of the polyhedra. Polyhedra are 3-dimensional objects whose faces have to be polygons.

Even though there are many different shaped polyhedra*, they all share a common property. To discover this connection, you will need to

*

Polyhedron means a many faced solid. Polyhedra is the plural form of this word.

count how many vertices (corners) it has, how many faces, and how many edges. Fill in the information in the chart.

Study the numbers carefully. Figure out the connection between the first two columns of numbers and the third column. Amazingly, it works out to be the same number for all polyhedra.

The discovery you will make here was written about by the famous mathematician Leonhard Euler in the 1700's.

regular polyhedron	number of faces	number of vertices	number of edges
tetrahedron	4	4	6
cube	....	....	....
octahedron	....	....	....
dodecahedron	....	....	....
icosahedron	....	....	....

The secret connection is given in the solutions section at the end of the book.

The golden rectangle dazzles Penrose

Penrose sat staring, as only a cat can, at a piece of paper with segments and a point drawn on it.

"I often wonder what that cat is thinking when he stares at something without even blinking?" wondered his mistress.

* * *

"Come back up here," pleaded a segment, "we've got to get busy and make more

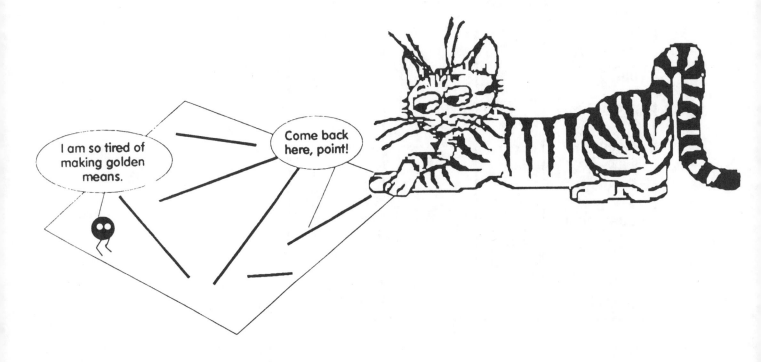

I am so tired of making golden means.

Come back here, point!

golden rectangles. Artists and architects are calling asking for sample rectangles to use in their works."

"But I am so tired of making golden means for the golden rectangles," replied the weary point. "Nature has demanded so many golden rectangles that just making the shape for many of its shells has been exhausting. Isn't there another way to make golden rectangles?" queried the point.

"I don't know of any," the segments all answered anxiously. "It can't be that much work for you to find the special location on each of us that divides our length into the golden mean."

"If you think it's so easy, you try it," said point angrily. "I have to do some very special and difficult computations each time to get that golden place, G, on each and every one of you. It's a lot of work to find the location on a segment so that G divides it into this ratio —

$$\frac{a}{b} = \frac{c}{a}$$

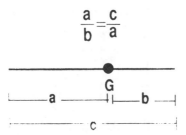

Penrose was totally mesmerized listening to all the different segments pleading with this

one point, G, to locate their golden means.

"What are you looking at?" the segments and the point asked Penrose, when they realized someone was staring at them.

"I think I can help you," Penrose replied. The segments and the point began to snicker, not believing a cat could help them.

Penrose was not discouraged and continued to speak, "I have watched how my mistress has made golden rectangles using squares."

"Squares?" they all shouted together.

"I have never heard of it," point replied skeptically, "but I am willing to listen, if it will help me."

Penrose began to explain— "Every golden rectangle can generate infinitely many golden rectangles inside itself by using squares, like this— "

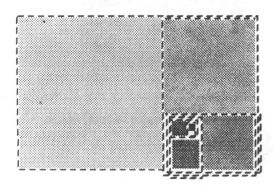

"Wow! that is impressive," they all exclaimed.

"Now watch how I can make a golden rectangle without any computation — just by using a square."

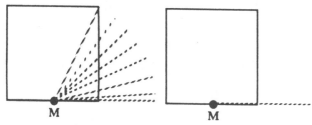

(1) Find the middle point, M, of this side of the square.

(2) Measure the distance from M to the corner of the square, as shown with the dotted line. Bring this distance down, as shown above.

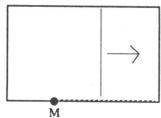

(3) Stretch the square out to the end of the dotted line, and form the golden rectangle.

"That's beautiful," the point marveled. "What else did you learn from your mistress' notes on the golden rectangles?" asked the point.

"Oh, many things, but the most exciting was how this beautiful equiangular spiral is hidden inside the golden rectangle," Penrose answered.

"Please show us," asked the segments and the point.

"So that's how nature uses the golden rectangle to make some of its shells," the point exclaimed.

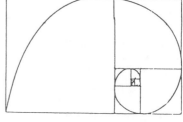

"You certainly helped us out, Penrose," the point added, and all the segments nodded in agreement.

Penrose suddenly felt all the segments and the point staring at him. "What is it?" he asked.

"Penrose, you are the golden cat !" the point declared. "You fit perfectly into this golden rectangle."

Sure enough, Penrose sat framed by a golden rectangle.

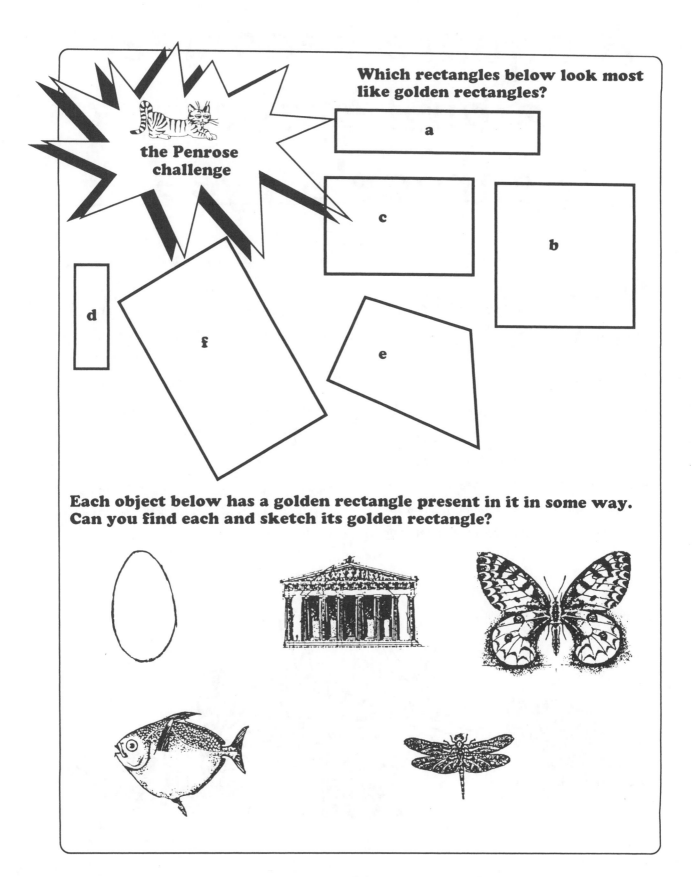

the Penrose challenge

Which rectangles below look most like golden rectangles?

a

c

b

d

f

e

Each object below has a golden rectangle present in it in some way. Can you find each and sketch its golden rectangle?

A square becomes a bird before Penrose's eyes

"What a gorgeous morning!" Penrose declared.

"It's time to check the morning sun." He stretched himself and then slowly sashayed into the living room. Penrose knew it would be full of sun at this time of the day. To his surprise square sheets of paper in all sizes were stacked all around the living room floor.

"Now what's she up to?" wondered Penrose. "My favorite spots are all occupied by her square sheets of paper. And there she is sitting on the floor folding up more squares. Well, I will just go plop myself down on top of the one she is working with," he thought. And sure enough, Penrose walked over boldly and stretched out right on top of his mistress' work.

"No, Penrose not now," she said. "I am right in the middle of making a bird." She lifted

Which of these do you like best?

him up and placed him in an unoccupied area near one of her creations. He glanced at her book, and saw the title— Origami. "Of course!" he realized, "she is doing origami."

"I remember the first time I discovered origami," he reminisced. "I had gone to visit Ms. Imagiro, the old lady with the kind voice. She always called after me when I walked by her house. In the beginning I was a bit scared. Then one day I saw her making things out of square pieces of paper. She had made all sorts of wonderful objects— a cat, an elephant, a camel, a hat, a box, birds.

So many things I can't remember them all. My curiosity got the best of me and before I knew it I was sitting next to her watching her hands move ever so quickly."

"So you like my creations, Penrose," she said. "You're such a pretty cat." With that statement I naturally began to purr. "Which of these do you like best?" she asked me. I reached out to the bird.

"I should have guessed," she replied. "Well, let me show you how to make it." And before my eyes she transformed the square sheet

37

of paper into a bird. To top it off she later
made me a bird whose wings flapped when
you pulled its tail.

Check the next page to see what I learned.
Why not try to make an orgami for yourself.

the Penrose challenge

• Below are the instructions for making a flying bird. It is difficult, but if you work slowly and carefully you'll make Penrose's favorite orgami.

• Go the the library and check out a book on origami. Discover the many things you can make.

• Get a book on paperfolding and learn such things as how to make a square sheet of paper from a rectangular one, and how to make a square appear within a square sheet of paper.

1. Take a square sheet of paper.

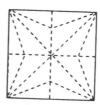

2. Make the creases shown by the dotted lines.

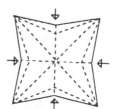

3. Fold in the parts where the arrows point.

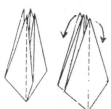

4. Fold the two flaps down.

5. Open flaps back.

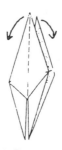

6. Fold flaps down.

7. Turn shape around.

8. Pull inside flaps out a little bit.

9. Make a head for the bird.

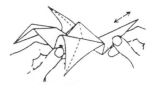

10. If you pull the tail of the bird back and forth, its wings will flap.

Penrose meets
Mr. Abacus

Mr. Abacus lived
down the street in
the big brown house
with all the stairs.

Penrose liked to visit different homes in the
neighborhood, but somehow he hadn't visited
the big brown house. The long flight of
stairs leading to the door seemed especially
intriguing today. The stream of sunshine on
the doormat was so inviting that Penrose
could not resist. He slowly climbed up the
flight of stairs, counting them as he went
along. At the top the sun's rays had
already warmed the mat, just as he'd
imagined they would have. He stretched out
on the mat. The warmth was just beginning
to penetrate his fur and soothe his body,
when the door creaked open. An old man
with a small white beard and mustache
looked down at him. "What have we here?"
asked the old man. "Such an elegant cat,"
he continued. Penrose did not move, for he

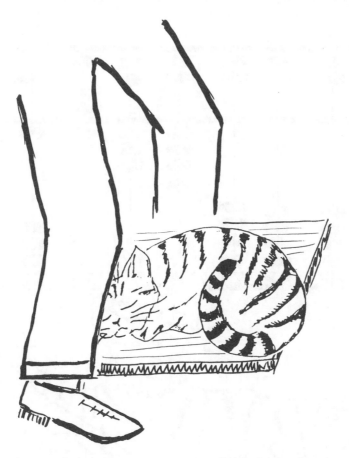

could sense the kindness of the old man. The old man bent down and began to pet Penrose, who couldn't help purring. Each knew he had made a new friend.

The old man, taking care not to disturb Penrose, stepped over him and sat on a nearby porch chair. In his hand he held a very interesting object. It was a wooden frame with wooden beads in columns. Penrose's cat curiosity was piqued. He couldn't resist. He got up and watched the old man as he moved the object's beads. "Ah, you want to know what this is," said the old man. "Yes," replied Penrose. "It looks like something I could do with my paws."

"Well, first let me introduce myself. I am Mr. Abacus, the world's oldest abacus user. I can do many mathematical things with the abacus."

"I am Penrose, the mathematical cat. I would be delighted if you would show me some of the things the abacus can do. Can you please show me?" Penrose asked.

Mr. Abacus was thrilled that Penrose was interested, so he decided to explain how numbers were represented on the abacus. "First, notice that there is a bar that separates a column of two beads from a column of five beads. Each column stands for a place value of a base ten number. For

example, the number 324 has 3 hundreds +
2 tens + 4 ones. So to show 324 on the

abacus, you use
the first three
columns in the
same order as
the number is
written—3
beads , 2 beads,
and then 4

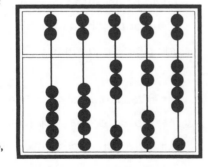

beads are pushed up to the dividing bar, like
this."

"But how are the columns of two beads
above the bar
used?" asked
Penrose.

Mr. Abacus
explained, "If
you had to

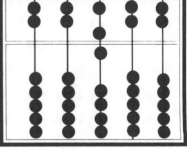

write the number 600, you would not have
enough beads in the third column of five
beads. So you pull down to the bar one bead
from the third two-bead column. Each bead
in the two-bead column is worth five of the

beads below it. By pulling down one of these beads you now have 500, so you need only one bead from the five-bead column to end up with 600. Here's what it looks like."

"Mr. Abacus, can you give me a number to do?" asked Penrose.

"Certainly. How about 4, 371?" asked Mr. Abacus.

Penrose sat and thought for a minute. Then he carefully moved the beads with his paws.

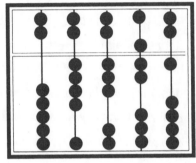

"Excellent!" enthused Mr. Abacus. "Here are some numbers for practice. The next time you visit we will learn how to add on the abacus."

"Thanks for the great lesson, Mr. Abacus. Now while you do your work, I'll go back to the mat to relax in the sun." Penrose drifted off to sleep feeling very proud that he had done his number correctly.

Answers are given in the solutions section at the end of the book.

Draw in beads on the abacus so the given number would be shown on the abacus.

3

9

37

254

Penrose discovers the mystery of the triangle of numbers

The first time I saw the triangle of numbers,

I thought it was just a design with numbers. I had gone over to visit Mr. Abacus. The door was ajar so I went in and jumped onto his table. There before me was a beautiful design. The more I stared at it the more I realized that it was more than just a design. There was something mathematical

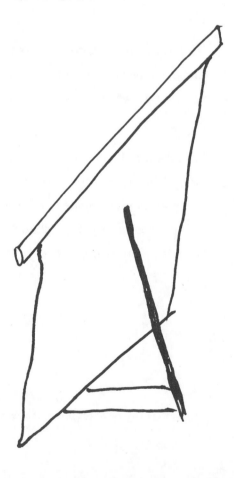

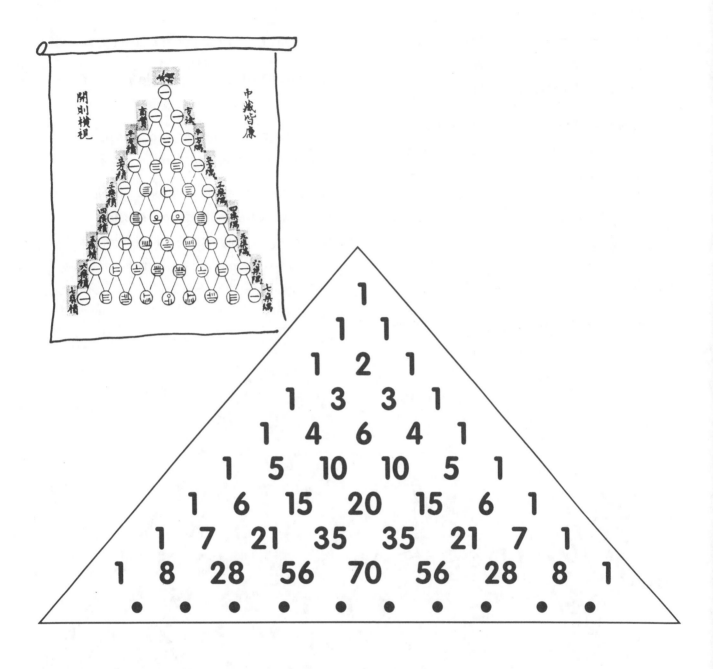

to it. As I studied it, I heard footsteps, and before I knew it Mr. Abacus was translating the figures in the triangle to numbers I recognized. "See, Penrose, this triangle of numbers is hundreds of years old. The oldest surviving book in which it appears dates back to 1303, and is written in Chinese. Do you recognize it now?" As he was rewriting it, I blurted out — "It's the Pascal triangle. I remember it from my mistress' book."

"Yes, that's what it has come to be called.

It was named after the mathematician Blaise Pascal who discovered many of its properties," Mr. Abacus explained.

"Properties?" I asked. "I only know how its numbers are formed. Each number is the result of adding the two numbers above it. For example, the circled 10 comes from adding the 4 and the 6 above the 10. What other properties does it have?"

"Oh, many," Mr. Abacus replied.

I was anxious to learn, remembering the time he taught me how to use the abacus.

"Look at the diagonal. What do you see?" he asked.

"Oh, a pattern," I replied, "and the next diagonal also has a pattern."

"Very good," he said encouragingly. "Now, let's discover something very special. Suppose you wanted to add the first five numbers along one of the dotted diagonals —for example, 1+3+6+10+15 — what would you do?" he asked.

"I guess I would get out my pencil and paper or calculator and add them up," I replied.

"Well, that is one way to do it, but this special triangle has the answer hidden in it," he said.

"Where?" I asked eagerly.

He pointed to the number below 15 and to the left. It was the number 35. He explained that this works for any diagonal and for as many numbers as you want to add.

"Amazing!" I declared. "This is a mathematical treasure."

"There are many more properties it possesses. It has properties involving probability, the Fibonacci numbers, powers of 11…many ideas are hidden in it — but we will discover those another time," he said smiling.

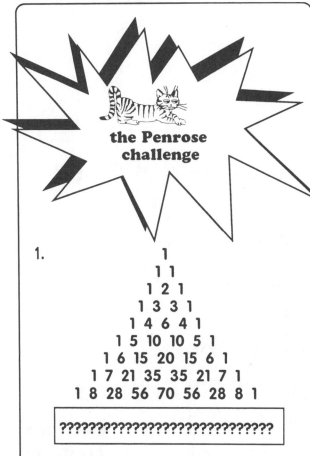

the Penrose
challenge

1.
```
            1
           1 1
          1 2 1
         1 3 3 1
        1 4 6 4 1
      1 5 10 10 5 1
     1 6 15 20 15 6 1
   1 7 21 35 35 21 7 1
 1 8 28 56 70 56 28 8 1
```

?????????????????????????

Fill in the numbers above that would be in the next row of this Pascal triangle.

Answers are given in the solutions section at the end of the book.

2. Go to your local library and see if you can find some additional information about the Pascal triangle.

Penrose meets the Tangramians

It was one of those rainy winter days. Penrose lay curled up in a ball-like shape on a pillow on the living room sofa.

His eyes were fixed on the pile of shapes on the coffee table. "Gee," thought Penrose, "humans amuse themselves in the strangest ways. For example, look at this pile of shapes." Penrose remembered watching his mistress

move the pieces around for hours while writing notes. "Very unusual, these humans," he thought, and gave a long yawn. Right in the middle of it he was startled by a voice. "Help me! Help me!" the voice

Help me! Help me! I am in disarray.

called. Penrose realized the voice was coming from the pile of shapes. "What is it?" shouted Penrose.

"I am in disarray," the pile replied.

"What are you?" Penrose asked.

"I am a Tangramian cat," the pile said.

"You don't look like a cat to me," Penrose thought.

"We were warned that any Tangramian who leaves Tangramia would fall in disarray," the pile continued.

"Wait a minute," Penrose interrupted. "I don't understand what you mean?"

"I come from the world of Tangramia. Everything in my world is formed from these seven shapes that come from a square," said the pile.

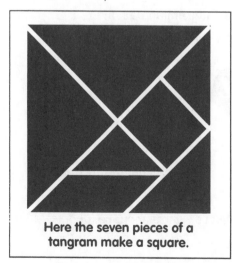

Here the seven pieces of a tangram make a square.

"It surely doesn't seem there could be many things in Tangramia. I doubt you could make many different things with just these seven pieces," said Penrose.

"Oh! to the contrary. There are thousands of different things in Tangramia. I happen to be a Tangramian cat, or should I say was?" The pile began to cry. "I didn't take heed and left Tangramia with your mistress. The legend warns that any object leaving Tangramia will fall in disarray—fall to pieces. And that's what happened to me. That's why I look like a pile of shapes. Please help me get myself back together and back to Tangramia." the pile pleaded.

"Me?" asked Penrose. "I have no idea how you should look or how these seven pieces go together."

"Please try," the Tangramian cat begged.

Penrose walked gingerly off his pillow onto the coffee table. He began pushing the pieces together in different ways with his paw. He tried to recall how his mistress played with the pieces. To his amazement he formed a cat's head with three of the pieces.

"Wonderful!" the Tangramian cat said excitedly. "Once I'm back in cat form I can leap back to Tangramia."

"But where is Tangramia?" asked Penrose.

"In your mistress' book, of course," replied the cat.

Stop playing with my tangram pieces.

Oh, thank you, thank you!

Penrose had to admit he was having fun feverishly batting the shapes to make a cat's form. Suddenly he felt his mistress' hands around his body. "Now what mischief are you getting into Penrose? Stop playing with my tangram pieces," she scolded. Just then the telephone rang and his mistress put him down to go to answer it. Naturally, Penrose seized the opportunity and immediately went back to work with the pieces of tangram. To Penrose's astonishment, he finally formed the shape of a cat.

"Oh, thank you, thank you," the Tangramian cat exclaimed. "Now I must leap back quickly in the book before your mistress returns. Perhaps someday you can visit our world." And the Tangramian cat disappeared into the pages of the book.

Penrose leaned over and gazed at the pages of the book. To his amazement there was the cat he had formed along with hundreds of other objects—birds, houses, people, boats, cats— almost anything you could imagine. All formed from the seven pieces of the tangram.

the Penrose challenge

Make a photocopy of this page and cut out the seven pieces forming the tangram square shown. Without looking at the square, can you make your pieces in the shape of the square, a triangle, a rectangle, a parallelogram?

Each of the five tangram figures below are made up of these seven pieces. Can you make each one?

Answers are given in the solutions section at the end of the book.

Penrose solves the case of the missing square

"Hello Watson,"
Penrose said,
greeting his old
friend.
"What are you doing?"

"Oh, I'm trying to figure out a problem,"
Watson replied. "My mistress has a
special 8 by 8 foot square platform made
in the following way."

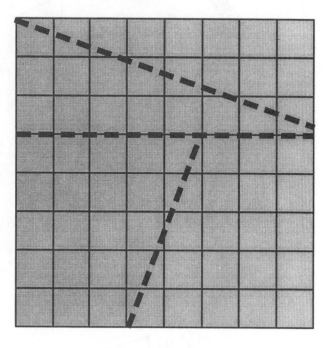

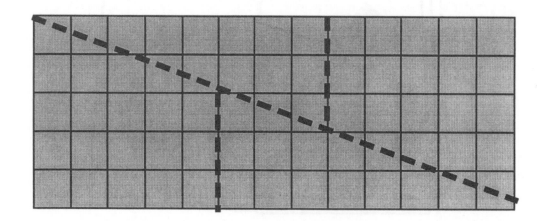

"What do those dotted lines represent?" Penrose asked.

"Oh, that means the square is made up of those four pieces," Watson answered confidently.

"Why did she want to make the square that way?" Penrose asked.

"Because she can shift the pieces around like this, and end up with a rectangle," Watson demonstrated.

"That's pretty clever," Penrose commented.

"I know," said Watson, "but there is one problem. The square is made up of 8 rows of 8 little squares. That is a total of 64 little squares. While the rectangle is made up of 5 rows of 13 little squares, for a total of 65 little squares. It seems that when the rectangle goes back into square form a little square is lost."

"Wow! This is definitely a problem for my Sherlock Holmes hat," Penrose said as he placed the hat upon his head.

Whenever Penrose wanted to tackle a really difficult logic problem he wore his Sherlock Holmes hat. Somehow the hat added to his confidence and he felt his logic skills improve. Wearing the hat, he made a model of the platform. He moved the pieces back and forth between the square form and the rectangular form. He took special care to inspect all the details of the problems. Watson watched as Penrose analyzed the problem. Penrose's eyes suddenly opened very wide, and Watson knew Penrose had solved the mystery.

To discover what Penrose found, make a photocopy of the square below. Then cut out the square, and cut the square along the dotted lines. Using the pieces form the rectangle . Study the rectangle. Can you discover what Penrose found out about the little missing square?

Look at the end of the book for a solution.

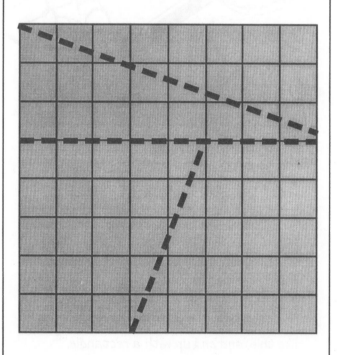

The invisible nanoworld

Penrose lay stretched out contemplating the ants rushing back and forth along a path near a daisy plant.

"Hey! you," shouted a voice, disturbing the silence Penrose was enjoying. Penrose turned to see from where the voice was coming. No one was in sight. "Hey, I'm lost. Where is Nanocity?" the voice asked in a

demanding tone. "I'm sorry. I can't see where you are," Penrose replied, "and I have never heard of or been to Nanocity."

"Of course you haven't. You're way too big. Nanocity is for the ultra small; all the nanos," the voice replied.

"Nanos?" Penrose questioned.

"Sure… nanoseconds, nanotools, nanotubes, nanobeings, even nanocats, like me."

"Like you? But you are invisible," Penrose said.

"Not invisible, just minute. You know how long a second is, right? Well, a nanosecond is one-billionth of a second. It is the unit used to measure time when working with computers because computers work so quickly. So a nanocat is one-billionth (1/1,000,000,000,000) the size of a cat like you. There is a whole new world of nanothings being created to deal and help with certain problems. The only limit to our use is imagination," the nanocat said.

"Can you give me an example?" Penrose asked the nanocat.

"People are now working on building tiny machinery which will be used to build even smaller machines, which will build even smaller ones until you get machines the size

56

you need for the jobs you want done," the nanocat replied.

"What jobs would be that small?" Penrose asked.

"You might want to make a nanocomputer. Or devise a type of decoy virus machine to stop certain diseases. The computer would be small enough to enter your body's blood stream. One could even make biological nanomachines to eat up hazardous waste molecules. The possibilities are many," nanocat said with a confident note to its voice.

"I see," Penrose said, "but how can something get so small?"

"Can't numbers be written smaller and smaller? For instance, 1/2 is smaller than 1. 1/3 is smaller than 1/2. 1/4 is smaller than 1/3. 1/5 is smaller than 1/4. And on and on. There is no end to how small numbers can get. The same could be true with things in nanoworld," nanocat

explained.

"So won't you help me find my way back?" nanocat asked.

"How can I help you if I can't even see you?" Penrose asked.

"Just point to the direction of your mistress' computer. I'll find a way to get back home," nanocat told Penrose.

"Her computer is in that room," Penrose said, pointing to his left.

"Thank you," nanocat replied, then added as its voice drifted away. "Perhaps, someday I'll become a celebrity like you and be a star in a nanocalendar."

...in that room.

Penrose loves the games numbers play

For many years Penrose had observed the way numbers operated.

Sometimes it seemed almost like magic, other times very tricky. Today Penrose was sitting on his mistress' special chess board. Instead of chess pieces she had made number pieces. It was midday and he had

58

the place to himself. Penrose gave one of his cat stretches, and his body reached clear across the chess board.

"Get off the board," yelled 2. "We have something to show you."

"What's up?" Penrose asked, a bit startled.

We want to set up the chess board so you can take a Knight's tour.

2

"We want to set up the chess board so you can take a **Knight's tour**," 2 answered.

"A Knight's tour?" Penrose wondered out loud.

"Just watch and you will see," 2 replied. The numbers began arranging themselves in this way:

1	48	31	50	33	16	63	18
30	51	46	3	62	19	14	35
47	2	49	32	15	34	17	64
52	29	4	45	20	61	36	13
5	44	25	56	9	40	21	60
28	53	8	41	24	57	12	37
43	6	55	26	39	10	59	22
54	27	42	7	58	23	38	11

"We are ready for you to take the Knight's tour," they all shouted from their positions on the board.

"I am ready, but how do I do it?" Penrose asked.

2 explained , "In chess a Knight moves like this — in the shape of an L. The way we have arranged ourselves you can move from the number 1 through to the number 64 using just the Knight's move. Try it."

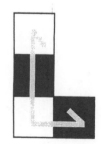

* * *

Penrose tried it and to his amazement, the Knight's move took him from 1 to 2 to 3 to 4 — all the way through the rest of the 64 numbers on the board. "Amazing!" Penrose blurted out.

• Try the Knight's tour for yourself. Here are the different shapes of the Knight's move.

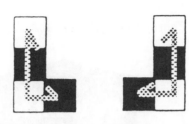

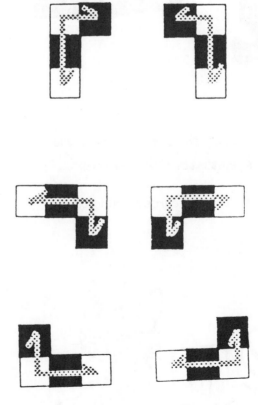

the Penrose challenge

• This 8x8 square of numbers is a special magic square. Each of the numbers in any row or column total the same amount. What amount is this?

1	48	31	50	33	16	63	18
30	51	46	3	62	19	14	35
47	2	49	32	15	34	17	64
52	29	4	45	20	61	36	13
5	44	25	56	9	40	21	60
28	53	8	41	24	57	12	37
43	6	55	26	39	10	59	22
54	27	42	7	58	23	38	11

• In addition, when this square is divided into four mini 4x4 squares, each of the columns and rows in the mini squares also add up to the same amount. What amount is this?

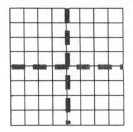

Answers are at the end of the book.

Penrose flips over the Möbius strip

Penrose tromped into the house. To his amaze-ment he found strips of paper strewn all over the living room floor. "Ah," he thought, "she's made me some toys." So he immediately began playing with the strips. He hit them with one paw then another, tossing them into the air. He was having a great time, but eventually he got tired. Noticing a sunny spot near the window, he decided to take one of his many afternoon cat naps. And, as usual, his imagination was a catalyst for a wild dream.

As Penrose drifted to sleep he found himself out in the yard ready to play with Augustus, the neighbor's kitten. Augustus leaped onto a large twisting ramp which seemed to appear out of nowhere. Penrose watched the kitten run inside it, and then suddenly run on top of it. Penrose was confused. How could Augustus be inside and atop the ramp without ever having to cross its edge? The only way to analyze this object was to take the plunge, and join Augustus. Penrose chased Augustus around and around the ramp. Sometimes he would be running on its floor and later on its ceiling, but he never crossed any corners or edges to get from the ceiling to the floor. How could this be?

He felt someone lifting him up. It was his mistress removing him from her models of Möbius strips. He realized he had been dreaming, and gave his usual cat stretch to help him wake up. Now he was ready to learn about some of the properties of the Möbius strip. Here are some of the ideas he discovered as he watched his mistress at work.

1) Let's compare three objects:

a) a strip of paper

b) a ring—a strip of paper with its ends glued together

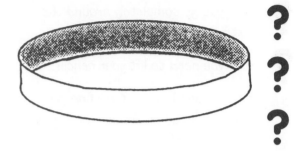

c) a Möbius strip—a strip of paper that is given a half twist and then its ends are glued together.

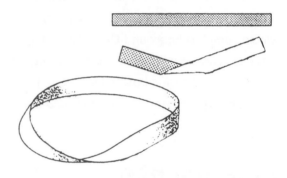

Imagine a spider crawling on the strip of paper or on the ring.

? • Can it get to the underside without crossing the edge?

If you answered no, you're correct.

Now imagine the sides on the Möbius strip. Try tracing the path of the spider with a pencil or crayon. Begin at one point of the strip.

•Did you get back to the starting point?

•Did you go completely around the strip?

•Did you need to lift your pencil?

• Yes. Yes. No. — You'll find your pencil can go all around the entire strip without lifting it.

One of the exciting things about the **Möbius strip** is that it was the first object discovered with only one side and one edge. If you trace your finger around the edge, you will go completely around the entire edge without having to lift your finger. A **ring** has two edges. To trace both edges, you must lift your finger to get to the untraced edge.

experiments _____

Here are some experiments you can do with the Möbius strip. You will need narrow strips of paper, a pair of scissors, and some transparent tape.

• experiment 1

1) Take a strip of paper. Draw a line down the center on each side. Now make a Möbius strip out of it by giving it a half twist and taping the ends together.

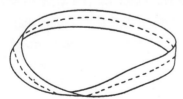

2) With your scissors cut the strip along the line you drew. What did you end up with?

3) You should have ended up with one long narrower ring shaped strip. Something like this—

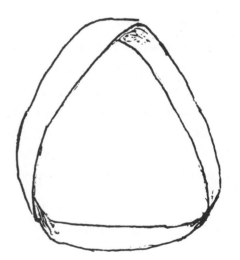

• experiment 2

Now guess what will happen if you cut the long narrow strip from step 3 again? Try it and find out. Were you surprised?

• experiment 3

Take a strip of paper and color a thick band, one-third its width down the center on each side.

With the scissors cut along the edge of the band you made.

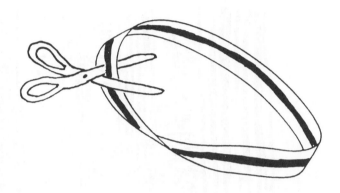

Make a new Möbius strip from this strip, as shown.

What do you think you'll get? Were you surprised?

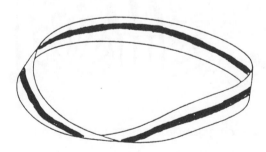

Penrose discovers mathematics in the forest

"What a fierce wind storm, Watson!"

Penrose declared, as the two cats walked in a grove of redwood trees.

"It certainly is," Watson replied. "Why do you think such gigantic trees produce such small sized cones?" Watson speculated. "And why so many thousands for each tree?" Watson asked Penrose.

"Believe it or not Watson, I think the answer lies in mathematics." Penrose replied, smiling.

"You seem to find mathematics in almost everything. Don't tell me this has to do with mathematics," Watson said, sounding exasperated.

"Let me explain why I think the answer lies with probability," Penrose began. " What is probability, you ask. It is a field of mathematics that calculates the likelihood of something happening. The chances of rain, the chances of winning an athletic event, the chances of winning an election, the chances of having fish for dinner—these are just a few of the areas where probability

when they are thrown. Notice how the tallest part of the stack shows the possible ways the number 7 can occur with two dice (1 & 6, 6 & 1, 2 & 5, 5 & 2, 3 & 4, 4 & 3). Since seven has the most number of ways of occurring, the chances of getting a 7 are greater."

"But how do you compute the probability of a seven coming up? And what does this have to do with redwood trees?" Watson asked.

"Look at the stacks of dice," Penrose continued. Count how many possible ways the two dice can land. What do you get?"

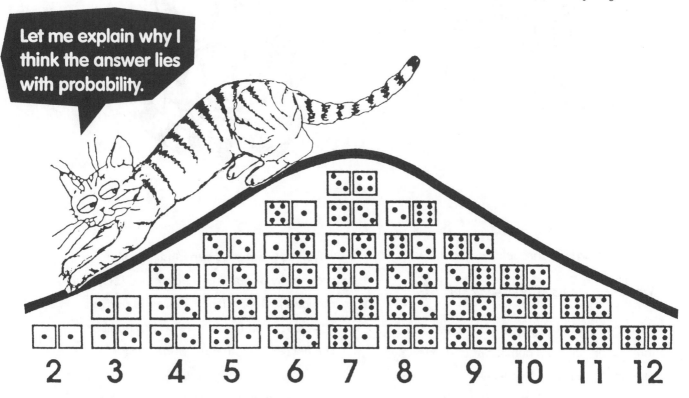

Let me explain why I think the answer lies with probability.

is at work. Look at these dice I have stacked up. These dice show all the possible combinations in which two dice can land

"I get 36 ways," Watson replied.

"Right!" Penrose declared. "How many ways

"But what does probability have to do with redwood trees and cones?"

The redwood tree produces thousands of cones with seeds, thereby increasing the probability of its seeds germinating and growing into a tree.

can 7 be made?" Penrose now asked.

"Why I see six ways," Watson said.

"Watson, probability is a fraction whose numerator tells the number of possible ways a desired event can happen—in this case getting a seven with two dice. And the denominator tells the number of all possible ways an event can occur—here all the 36 ways that two dice can land. So the probability of getting a seven is 6/36, which reduces to 1/6. Either answer is correct. The closer the fraction is to the number 1, the better the chances of an event happening," Penrose explained. " That's just one of many mathematical ideas behind probability."

"But what does this have to do with

redwood trees and cones?" Watson was getting impatient.

"Just think Watson, how nature tries to preserve a balance of plants and animals. A balance that provides food and habitat for all species, Penrose began.

"Yes, I understand that," Watson replied.

"It is an amazing job," Penrose continued ignoring Watson's reply. "Since it is very difficult for a redwood seedling to survive to adulthood, nature improves its chances by having the redwood tree produce thousands of cones with seeds, thereby increasing the probability of seeds germinating and growing into a tree."

"That's amazing," Watson replied astonished. "I never thought of it that way."

"Imagine, Watson, each cone of the redwood tree is bewteen 1/2" and 1" long and carries 80 to 130 seeds which remain fertile for as long as 15 years," Penrose explained.

"Really?" Watson was trully surprised.

"In fact Watson, a giant redwood tree produces several million seeds per year. So you see, through the numbers and sizes of seeds, nature enhances the probability of a seed's germination. Even after a redwood seed germinates, the probability of it developing into a mature redwood tree is 1 out of several thousands."

"So that's how mathematics and redwood trees are linked," Watson said.

"Watson, let's just say that is **one** way they are connected," Penrose responded with a grin.

"I should have known," Watson said, as they walked away.

Penrose meets Lo-shu

It was one of those hot summer days when even a cat sought a shady place away from the sun's bright rays.

Penrose was stretched out on the cool green grass his mistress had just watered. The drops felt so refreshing against his fur.

Suddenly he was startled. The rock on which he had rested his paw began to move. "What's happening?" he wondered. Then he realized the rock had grown a head, four legs and a tail, and was moving. "What are you?" asked Penrose. "What do you mean,'What am I?' I am Lo-shu the tortoise."

"Lo-shu is not a tortoise," replied Penrose. "It's a special magic square with numbers from 0 to 9."

"I know," said the tortoise. "I am the divine tortoise that carried the first magic square on my back along the bank of the Yellow river to Emperor Yu of China. The year was 2200 B.C."

"But where's your magic square now?" asked Penrose.

"The Emperor took it from me, and never gave it back," said Lo-shu. "I've wandered all over the world in search of another magic square. You are a good omen. You are the first animal I ever met to know what lo-shu is. Can you help me get my magic square back?"

"No problem," said Penrose, and he immediately began writing numbers on the tortoise's shell. "I've read all about magic squares. I even know a way to make your magic square. I know that the numbers from 1 to 9 are arranged in the square so that any row, column or diagonal of three totals 15. That is one of the magic properties of a magic square. I can show you exactly how I did this."

"That would be great, Penrose. So if anything happens to my magic square, I can put the numbers back," Lo-sho replied as he sauntered ever so slowly across the grass.

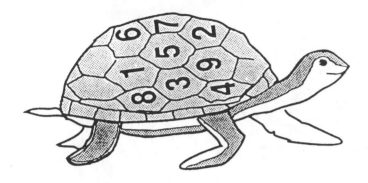

Here's Penrose's method for making 3x3, 5x5, 7x7, or any odd-sided magic square.

— STEPS —

The diagrams show a 3x3 magic square being made with the numbers 1 throught 9.

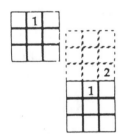

1) Always start by placing the first number in the middle box of the top row.

2) Make or imagine squares around the magic square. As you are placing numbers they will sometimes land in these squares. If a number lands in a box in an imaginary square, place that number in the same location of the magic square.

3) Each number is placed diagonally upward in the next box. If it lands in a box of an imaginary square, relocate it in the magic square.

4) If the diagonally upward box has a number in it, place the new number below the last number written in the magic square.

5) Repeat steps (3) and (4) until all the numbers have been placed.

Using the numbers 1, 2, 3, 4, 5, 6, 7, 8, 9, 10, 11, 12, 13, 14, 15, 16, 17, 18, 19, 20, 21, 22, 23, 24, 25 **make a 5 by 5 magic square using the method that Penrose used. The first step has been entered.**

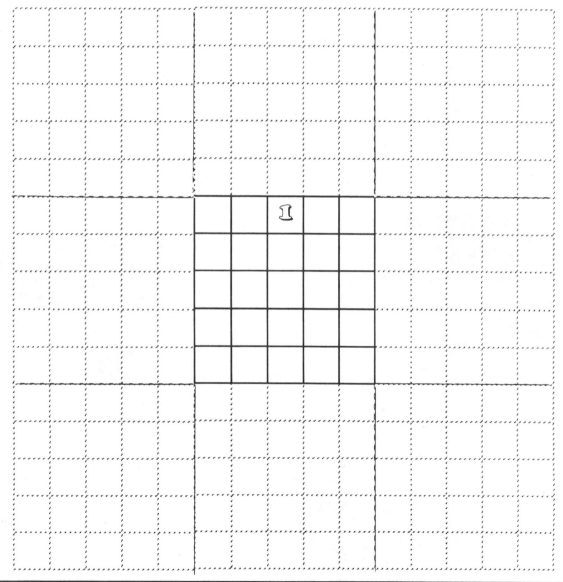

Mauritus teaches Penrose a tessellation trick

Penrose often wondered why Mauritus wore a beret, even though he was not a French cat.

Today as Mauritus sashayed by, Penrose asked, "How is it I always see you wearing a beret, Mauritus?"

"Because I am an artist, Penrose. It seems to help inspire me," Mauritus replied. "For the same reason you sometimes wear your Sherlock Holmes hat when you have a tough logic problem to tackle, I wear my beret."

" I would love to see some of your work, Mauritus," Penrose posed.

"Well, follow me," Mauritus directed, and Penrose followed as Mauritus led the way.

Mauritus had his very own art studio and house.

There on the walls of his cat-apartment, Mauritus had created fascinating designs that fit together beautifully. "Very impressive," Penrose marveled. Penrose recognized the designs as tessellations, similar to some he had seen in a book about the artist M.C. Escher on his mistress' desk.

"Are these wonderful designs difficult to create, Mauritus?" Penrose asked.

"Not for me Penrose, because I have mastered some of the many tessellating techniques," Mauritus replied.

"Can you explain how you created some of these?" Penrose asked eagerly.

"Why, of course. Here, let me let me show you how I made this one." And Mauritus began to draw.

"The secret to doing this is to know that certain objects tessellate a plane. They cover the plane like tiles, leaving no gaps. I discovered that equal sized rectangles are great for making tessellation designs. What I do is take a rectangle and transform it, and use this new shape to tessellate the plane. Here's an example."

Take any size rectangle with which you are comfortable.

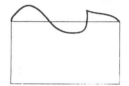

Tranform its top side in any way you want.

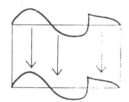

Now shift that same design to the bottom side.

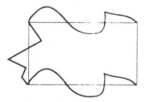

Now transform the rectangle's left side.

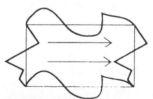

Shift that design to the right side.

I use the shape I made as a template. Then I duplicate it and shade a pattern, like this one. Notice how the shapes fit together perfectly. Voilà! We have a tesselation.

This is very impressive Mauritus. I am going to try one myself.

76

Tessellations are studied in mathematics. Certain geometric shapes tessellate while others do not. For example, a square tessellates because identical squares can fit together to cover a flat surface without overlapping or leaving any holes. On the other hand, identical shapes of a pentagon cannot tessellate. When placed side by side they do not fit together perfectly, and gaps exist. The **square**, the **equilateral triangle** (all sides the same length) and the **regular hexagon** (all six sides and six angles the same size) can be used to tessellate a plane. The honeycomb is an example of how nature uses the hexagon to tessellate.

the Penrose math ideas

the Penrose challenge

• Now try out your own tessellation creation. Choose or make shapes that tessellate a sheet of paper.

•After you have made different tessellating shapes and created you own designs, why not go to your local library or look on the internet for information on tessellations. You might also want to look at some of the wonderful tessellations in the works of the artist M.C. Escher. See if you can learn about other ways to make tessellations.

Look at the end of the book for a solution.

Penrose discovers Penrose

"I recognize some of this," thought Penrose. "I've seen her tessellate beautiful repeating patterns with squares, triangles, hexagons. "Hmmmm.

Interesting," Penrose mused as he pawed through a new article his mistress was working on. Suddenly a big cat grin came across his face when he noticed the title of the article was Penrose tiles. "She named these tiles after me," he purred proudly. But as he read on, to his amazement, he

She named these tiles after me.

Penrose tiles

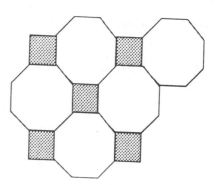

These two simple shapes can be used to tessellate.

discovered there is a mathematician and physicist named Roger Penrose. "So he is the one who discovered these two tiles. Then she must have named me after him, since I too am rather clever at mathematics."

His cat curiosity got the best of him, and Penrose began reading his mistress' article. "This is fascinating," he thought. "These two simple shapes can be used to tessellate (tile a flat surface and not leave gaps) in designs that never repeat one another. I remember when my mistress used

octagons and squares to tessellate, but the design continually repeated itself." In his mind he visualized what she had done.

"Now let me see how these two shapes tessellate," Penrose said as he began to move pieces his mistress had on her desk. "One is shaped like a dart and one looks like a kite," he noticed. To his surprise he

lined them up, as shown, the pattern repeated itself.

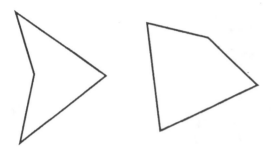

Penrose must have spent at least an hour making designs then rearranging them, before his mistress walked in. "Into my work again, Penrose?" she said. "I've never heard of a cat that liked math as much as you. And what a coincidence that you are playing with Penrose tiles, as if you knew their name." Penrose walked up to his mistress and rubbed against her hand and an enormous purr erupted inside him.

realized that is what they were named. He began pushing darts and kites together, and the designs in the tessellation did not repeat. Then he discovered if he made a rhombus with the dart and kite and just

the Penrose challenge

Using the dart and kite below as stencils, make at least thirty of each shape. Then, begin fitting them together, and discover the different patterns you can make.

Penrose tiles dart & kite stencils

Penrose tangles with the impossible figures

Penrose is a very curious cat.

Whenever his mistress was away and her office door was closed, he knew something new was taking place. Little did his mistress know that a closed door could not contain Penrose's curiosity. So today, as on other days, he stood on his back paws and pushed with his front paws, and the bifold door cracked open. Nudging the door with his nose he was able to slither through the narrow opening.

"Just as I thought," Penrose said out loud. "A new project to tantalize me. This is a strange looking model. It's made out of wood. And the drawing she made of it makes my mind and eyes jump back and forth."

Continuing to look at it, he speculated, "Why don't the ends of this wooden model connect?" Yet he noticed when he walked to another part of the room and looked at it from a different perspective it looked like the drawing with all its ends connected. "Very strange." He decided he had to look at her notes because what he saw was very confusing.

Jumping onto her desk, two words from her notes stood out — **impossible figures.**

"Impossible figures — what does she mean by that? Is this model an impossible figure? If so, why?" His mind was being flooded with questions. "The only way to understand what she is doing is to analyze this from a mathematical point of view," he decided. So he jumped down and began some serious thinking.

"I can see the object drawn on paper, and it looks real. But the model she made does not end up being exactly like the drawing. Why?......

"Because not all the ends of the models can be joined together. Let me look again at the the drawing she calls the **tribar.** On paper it looks like a very thick sided triangle. But the model's three sides can't be joined

together.
… I see each
of its angles
is a right
angle or 90°.
…
Hmmmmm
… That's
it!!!" Penrose
shouted.
"That's it!
… I know
from
geometry
the three
angles of
any triangle
total exactly
180°, but if

the tribar

the four-bar

the **tribar** has three right angles that
totals 270° (90°+90°+90°) — which is
impossible in Euclidean geometry. Ha, ha!…

"When I saw the model on paper, it was
distorted so the ends could meet. But the
wooden model's ends did not meet as in a
triangle. They only appeared to meet when I
viewed it from afar and at a particular angle
so the two disjoined ends **only appeared** to
be connected."

Penrose was very excited by his discoveries.
He decided to tackle the second figure his

mistress had drawn, labeled a
four-bar. Studying the drawing
of the figure he noticed it was
supposed to be made up of two
parallel bars (the vertical ones)
and two horizontal bars which
crossed each other at right
angles. "Why isn't this possible?"
He thought, and thought, and
thought. He looked, and looked,
and looked at the drawing.
Suddenly a big smile came
across Penrose's face. He had
the answer. "If I were to make a
model of this drawing, the top
and bottom bars would twist the
parallel vertical bars and they
would no longer remain parallel.
They would be skewed.* He felt
proud of himself for having solved that
problem. He gave forth a gigantic purr, and
stretched out in the sunshine streaming in
on the office floor. The warm sun rays
overcame his mathematical curiosity, and
he fell asleep purring.

*Skew
lines
are
lines
that do
not intersect, and do not
lie on the same flat
surface. They crisscross
but are apart. Parallel
lines do not intersect,
and lie on the same flat
surface.

Which objects below are impossible figures?

a.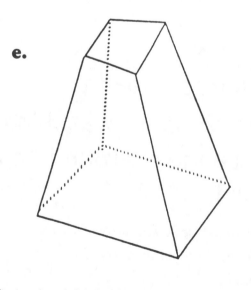

b.

c.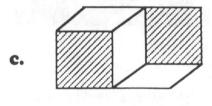

e.

d.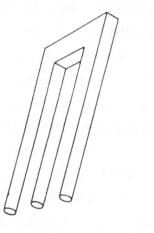

(Look at the end of the book for a solution.)

85

Penrose learns more number antics

Okay, I want the numbers from 1 to 64 on the checker board.

Penrose used to spend hours watching ants move around the yard.

But ever since he was introduced to numbers, he loves to observe their antics instead.

"I learn so much by watching the games

numbers play. They always introduce me to different number games. For example, yesterday they were breaking themselves into prime factors and looking for common multiples. Then they started making new magic squares. This morning they started changing themselves into different bases. Sometimes they change so quickly, I miss how and what they did. Then I have to go back and think about it, until I figure it out. Right now they seem to be starting to warm up with something familiar."

"Okay," directed 1, "Let's have the digits from 1 to 8 line up in a column in descending order, right here." 1 pointed to the line up spot. "Now, do the same in a column right next to it, but in ascending order. Perfect," 1 yelled. Penrose immediately recognized their formation as an easy way for the 9 times tables.

1 8	= 2x9
2 7	= 3x9
3 6	= 4x9
4 5	= 5x9
5 4	= 6x9
6 3	= 7x9
7 2	= 8x9
8 1	= 9x9

But 1 didn't stop directing. "Okay, now I want the numbers from 1 to 64 on the checker board. Right now. But this time 1 through 8 line up on the bottom row from left to right, then 9 through 15 on the next row from right to left, the 16 to 25 on the next row up from left to right, and so on."

"Well that's interesting," Penrose thought. I've never seen them lineup like that before. When they were all in order, they turned to Penrose and shouted—"Well, how do we look?"

"Great, but what's your game?" Penrose asked.

"You have to discover the magic of this

Well, how do we look?

Great, but what's your game?

arrangement for yourself Penrose," I said, wanting to tantalize Penrose's curiosity.

Penrose immediately took out his pencil and began to look for patterns. Follow Penrose's steps and discover what he found.

step 1 — How many squares in half the length of this checkerboard? Put this same number in each of the blank spaces of column A.

step 2 — Add the two centermost numbers in each row, and place that number in that row's blank space in column B.

step 3 — Multiply the numbers in column A and B, and place the product in column C.

step 4 — Find the differences between each row of the numbers in column C, and put that number in row D's blank space.

What do you notice about column D? Right! All the numbers in column D are 64, which is the number of squares in this checkerboard.

64	63	62	61	60	59	58	57
49	50	51	52	53	54	55	56
48	47	46	45	44	43	42	41
33	34	35	36	37	38	39	40
32	31	30	29	28	27	26	25
17	18	19	20	21	22	23	24
16	15	14	13	12	11	10	9
1	2	3	4	5	6	7	8

A	B	C	D
	61+60	4x121	
4	121	484	

Penrose problems

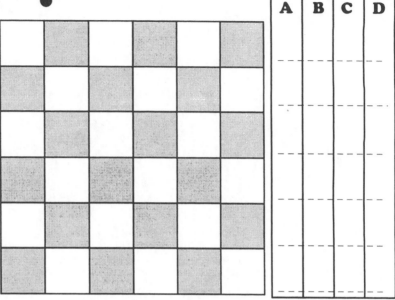

A	B	C	D

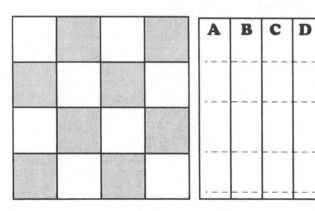

A	B	C	D

2. Do the same steps for a 4 by 4 checkerboard using the numbers from 1 to 16. What does column D come out to be?

3. For a 3 by 3 and a 5 by 5 checkerboard, column B's numbers are found in a different way. Its numbers are simply the numbers in the center column of the square. The rest of the process is the same. Try it out.

An example is given in the solution section at the back of the book.

solutions & answers section

answers & solutions to questions & challenges

Page 3_____

1011 in base two is written as follows:

1 eight+**0** fours +**1** two +**1** one = 11
  8   + 0   + 2   + 1

Page 7_____

Here are some square root
problems to try.

example: $\sqrt{9}$ =3 because 3 x 3 = 9.

(1) $\sqrt{16}$ = **4**

(2) $\sqrt{49}$ = **7**

(3) $\sqrt{25}$ = **5**

(4) $\sqrt{1}$ = **1**

(5) $\sqrt{64}$ = **8**

(6) Can you express the number $\sqrt{8}$
as a fraction? **No, because it is an
irrational number. These numbers
cannot be written as fractions, nor
can they be exactly expressed by
decimals.**

Page 9_____

How do **even** and **odd** sided polygon stars form?

• The odd sided polygon's stars can be formed
without lifting your pencil up when connecting
alternating vertex points of the polygon.

• With the even sided polygon, two figures are
drawn which lie on top of each other. The pencil
must be lifted to draw each figure.

How can you tell how many points a polygon's star will have?

• It will have the same number as the number of
sides of the polygon.

answers & solutions to questions & challenges

Page 11_____

What Penrose discovered about Pancake world.

Penrose discovered the world of only two dimensions. Everything in this world exists only on a flat surface. The inhabitants of Pancake world are perfectly flat. They can only see the two dimensions of any object or thing. This explains why the Δ thought Penrose looked like the impression of his paws prints. The Δ was not able to look up, since it was confined to the flat world. It and all other creatures of this world can only move along its flat surface, so they move only in the directions of forward, backward, and sideways. They can't move in or out or up or down. When Penrose picked up the Δ's house, he lifted it out of the Δ's world, and that is why the Δ began to panic. To the Δ, its house had disappeared.

Page 15_____

The 4th stage of the fractal looks like this:

answers & solutions to questions & challenges

Page 19_____

In which objects below do triple junctions appear? In all of them.

a) On the fish, triple junction appears in how the scales come together.

b) On the corn, look closely how the kernels are crowded together. You will notice triple junction here.

c) On the tortoise's shell the plates come together at triple junctions.

d) If you peel open the banana and slice a round piece, you will discover triple junction. The sliced pieces come apart in three identical sections. See the diagram below.

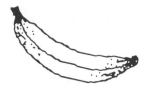 

e) The cells of the honeycomb are hexagons. They also come together in triple junctions.

Page 21_____

Questions about the pentagon. Here is how the diagonals appear in the pentagon. Notice the five-pointed star and the new pentagon inside it.

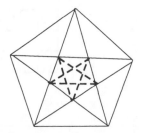

• When you draw in the diagonal on the new pentagon, a new five-pointed star (a pentagram) appears.
• You can draw in pentagons forever.
• Everytime you draw in the diagonals of the pentagon, a new pentagram appears, and within it a new pentagon appears.

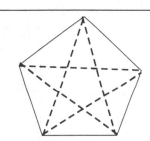

answers & solutions to questions & challenges

Page 25_____

Finding Fibonacci numbers in flowers.

cosmos has _8 petals_

trillium has _3 petals_

wild rose has _5 petals_

bloodroot has _8 petals_

Page 27_____

Here is how to make the puzzling egg and its birds.

answers & solutions to questions & challenges

Page 31_____

Discovering the secret connection of the polyhedra

Studying the chart that you filled in, notice that the first two columns always add up to 2 more than the third column.

regular polyhedron	number of faces	number of vertices	number of edges
tetrahedron	4	4	6
cube	6	8	12
octahedron	8	6	12
dodecahedron	12	20	30
icosahedron	20	12	30

The secret connection is:

faces + vertices = edges +2

Page 35_____

- Rectangles **c** and **f** are golden rectangles.
- Here are the golden rectangles in the objects below.

Page 43

Here's how the beads on the various abaci would appear for these numbers.

3

9

37

254

Page 47

1.

```
                    1
                  1   1
                1   2   1
              1   3   3   1
            1   4   6   4   1
          1   5  10  10   5   1
        1   6  15  20  15   6   1
      1   7  21  35  35  21   7   1
   ⓪  1   8  28  56  70  56  28   8   1   ⓪
   1   9  36  84 126 126  84  36   9   1
```

The numbers in the next row of this Pascal triangle are shown in the rectangle. Each number is the sum of the two numbers in the row above it, for example 1+8=9.

97

Here is how the various objects are made using the seven pieces of the tangram.

Here is how the rectangle is made, and what Penrose found out about the little missing square.

When the pieces of the cut up square are carefully put together, you will see a gap between them. This gap totals one square of the checkerboard.

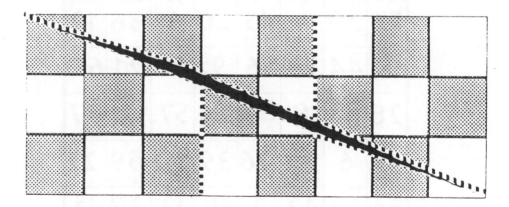

• Each of the numbers in any row or column total 260.

1	48	31	50	33	16	63	18
30	51	46	3	62	19	14	35
47	2	49	32	15	34	17	64
52	29	4	45	20	61	36	13
5	44	25	56	9	40	21	60
28	53	8	41	24	57	12	37
43	6	55	26	39	10	59	22
54	27	42	7	58	23	38	11

• When this square is divided into four mini 4x4 squares, each of the columns and rows in the mini squares also add up to the same amount which is 130.

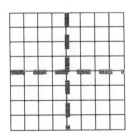

Page 64_____

• **experiment 2**
After cutting along the narrow strip from step 3, you end up with 2 strips that are linked together.

• **experiment 3**
Cutting along the edge of the band, you end up with two strips linked. The smaller one has the thick band on it.

Page 77_____

• **tessellating with a square**

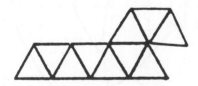

• **tessellating with an equilateral triangle**

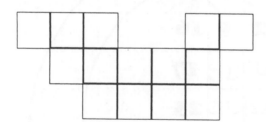

• **tessellating with a hexagon**

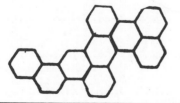

Here is how the numbers 1, 2, 3, 4, 5, 6, 7, 8, 9, 10, 11, 12, 13, 14, 15, 16, 17, 18, 19, 20, 21, 22, 23, 24, 25 **end up appearing in a 5 by 5 magic square using the method that Penrose used.**

A number landing in an imaginary square is relocated to its same place in the magic square. The arrows illustrate this for 2, 4, and 9.

Recall whenever a place in the magic square is occupied by another number, the new number landing there must be written under the last number that was put down. This is what happened to 16. 16 cannot be put in its place in the magic square because this location is already occupied by 11. Therefore, 16 must be placed under the last number written, namely 15.

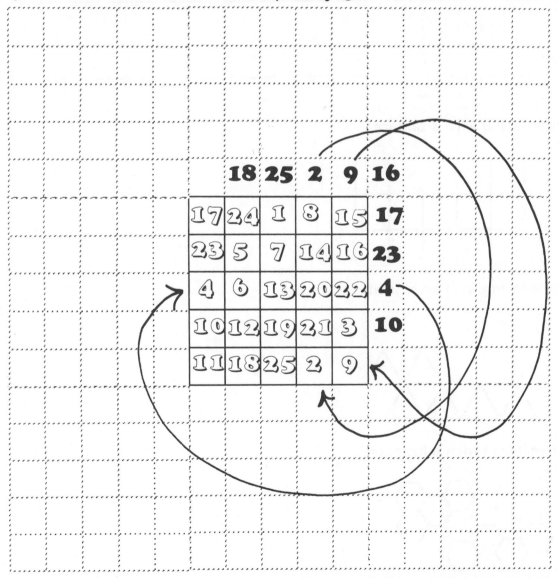

a. (a) is impossible. If you look at the object as stairs and imagine you were walking around it in the clockwise direction, you would always be going up the stairs even though you are going around in a circle. Someone walking around counterclockwise would always be going downstairs.

b. (b) is an actual 2-dimensional object.

c. (c) is an impossible figure, which is an optical illusion of two squares that seem to move inward and outward as we stare at it.

d. (d) is an impossible figure. It appears to have three prongs, but when you cover the lower part it seems to have only two prongs. It is an optical illusion.

e. (e) is impossible. When the edges of this 3-dimensional object are extended they should meet at one point and form a pyramid, but they do not.

Page 88_____

1. For a 6 by 6 checkerboard, all the numbers in column D come out to be 36, which is the number of squares in a 4 by 4 square.

2. For a 4 by 4 checkerboard, all the numbers in column D come out to be 16, which is the number of squares in a 4 by 4 square.

31	32	33	34	35	36
25	26	27	28	29	30
19	20	21	22	23	24
13	14	15	16	17	18
7	8	9	10	11	12
1	2	3	4	5	6

A	B	C	D
3	67	201	
3	55	165	36
3	43	129	36
3	31	93	36
3	19	57	36
3	7	21	36

Here is how a 5 by 5 square works.

3. Here is how the 5 by 5 checkerboard works. 25 is the number of squares in a 5 by 5 checkerboard.

21	22	23	24	25
16	17	18	19	20
11	12	13	14	15
6	7	8	9	10
1	2	3	4	5

A	B	C	D
		C=A xB	
5	23	115	25
5	18	90	25
5	13	65	25
5	8	40	25
5	3	15	

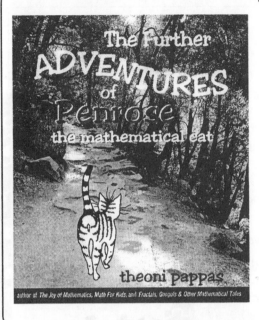

FRACTALS, GOOGOLS
and Other Mathematical tales

A treasure trove of Penrose's adventures and other stories that make mathematical ideas come to life. Explore math concepts with Penrose the cat, and other mathematical characters— such as π, the numberline, Leonhard the magic turtle, the googols, Fibonacci rabbit. Offers an amusing and entertaining way to explore and share mathematical ideas regardless of age or math background.

$10.95 • 64 pages • ISBN:0-933174-89-6

THE ADVENTURES OF PENROSE
The Mathematical Cat
by Theoni Pappas

Join Penrose on a madcap tour of mathematical ideas.
- Venture with him when he discovers how to help the square root of 2
- Meet the fractal dragon
- Watch a tangram egg hatch
- learn how to make a square become a bird
- Help nanocat get back home
- and many more amusing, entertaining and informative tales.

All told in an enchanting and captivating style that is sure to make mathematics fun as well as educational. The reader will gain new insights and appreciation for mathematics and its many facets.

$10.95 • 128 pages • ISBN:1-884550-14-2

MATH FOR KIDS &
OTHER PEOPLE TOO!
by Theoni Pappas

A book that brings mathematics to life in stories, puzzles and challenges.

Here we —
- find how the fractions were squeezed between the whole numbers
- witness the rise and fall of the Roman numerals
- do mental gymnastics with intriguing puzzles
- challenge a friend to a special game
- help factorials cut things down to size
- discover what's a zillion
- learn the magic of binary cards
- and much much more

Helps kids find out that mathematics is more than just computation.

Lets them discover the world of mathematics.

$10.95 • 128 pages • ISBN:1-884550-13-4

107

other mathematics books by theoni pappas

THE MAGIC OF MATHEMATICS
by Theoni Pappas

Delves into the world of ideas, explores the spell mathematics casts on our lives, and helps you discover mathematics where you least expect it.

"Thought-provoking yet not overwhelming, this book makes the author's pleasure in mathematics evident. " —**Library Journal**

"…witty and intriguing…" —**Science News**

"Readers will relish this book. The focus is to explain math in a lively, revealing manner. It succeeds!" —**The Bookwatch**

"Pappas writes at a level that puts all her topics within reach of any mathematics teacher and usually within reach of a generalist as well. In spite of this, she does not skim over facts or misrepresent them. If you haven't bought Pappas' first two books, then get them. If you have them, buy this one as well. —**TheMathematics Teacher**

$12.95 •8.5"x5.5"• 324 pp
• photos & illustrations throughout
• ISBN:0-933174-99-3

Selected by
QUALITY PAPERBACK BOOK CLUB®
Book-of-the-MONTH CLUB

MATH STUFF
by Theoni Pappas

Whether it's stuff in your kitchen or garden, stuff that powers your car or your body, stuff that helps you work, communicate or play, or stuff that you've never heard of – you can bet that mathematics is there.

MATH STUFF brings it all in the open in the Pappas style.

Learn what a holyhedron is, how computers get stressed, how e-paper will work, how codes and numbers work with our bodies. Learn about up-to-date math ideas and how they will impact our lives.

By the end of this book, you will think mathematics is the "stuff that dreams are made of."

$12.95 • 8.5"x5.5" • 224 pp
• photos & illustrations throughout
• ISBN:1-884550-26-6109

THE MUSIC OF REASON
THE BEAUTY OF MATHEMATICS THROUGH QUOTATIONS
by Theoni Pappas

Learn what Alice in Wonderland, Albert Einstein, William Shakespeare, Mae West, Plato and others have to say about mathematics.

THE MUSIC OF REASON is a compendium of profound and profane thoughts on mathematics by mathematicians, scientists, authors and artists.

"The collection of quotes is divided into fifteen categories…each preceded by a short commentary… (which) act as a springboard for some lively discussions linking mathematics to other subjects and to the real world. This amusing little book will complement the collection of mathematicians and mathematics educators alike. —**The Mathematics Teacher**

$9.95
• 138 pp
• ISBN: 1-884550-045

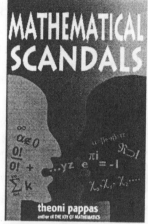
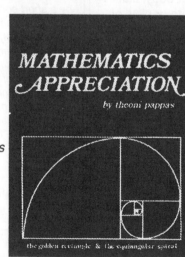

110

About Penrose

Penrose first decided to study mathematics when it was becoming increasingly impossible to get his mistress' attention. Whenever she would work on some project, he knew he would be neglected. He tried everything, from clawing furniture to pretending he was sleeping on her papers. Nothing seemed to work once she began reading her math books. Instead of moping around and feeling sorry for himself, he decided there must be something to this mathematics in which his mistress absorbed herself. He began to read the books she'd leave around. Penrose became fascinated with the ideas he read, and today he looks forward to math project time.

Penrose curled up on his mistress' desk while thinking about mathematics.

Theoni Pappas

About the Author

Mathematics teacher and consultant Theoni Pappas received her B.A. from the University of California at Berkeley in 1966 and her M.A. from Stanford University in 1967. Pappas is committed to demystifying mathematics and to helping eliminate the elitism and fear often associated with it. In 2000 she received *The Excellence in Achievement Award* from the University of California Alumni Association.

Many of her books have been translated into Japanese, Finnish, Slovakian, Czech, Korean, traditional & simplified Chinese, Turkish, Italian, Portuguese, Russian, French, Thai, and Spanish.

Her innovative creations include *The Mathematics Calendar, The Math-T-Shirt, The Children's Mathematics Calendar, The Mathematics Engagement Calendar,* and *What Do You See?*—an optical illusion slide show with text. Pappas is also the author of the following books: *Mathematics Appreciation, The Joy of Mathematics, Greek Cooking for Everyone, Math Talk, More Joy of Mathematics, Fractals, Googols and Other Mathematical Tales, The Magic of Mathematics, The Music of Reason, Mathematical Scandals, The Adventures of Penrose —The Mathematical Cat, Math for Kids & Other People Too!,* and *Mathematical Footprints.* Her most recent books are *Math-A-Day, Math Stuff,* and *The Further Adventures of Penrose the Mathematical Cat.*